Roaring Brook Press is a division of Holtzbrinck Publishing Holdings Limited Partnership, 175 Fifth Avenue, New York, New York 10010
All rights reserved

Distributed in Canada by H. B. Fenn and Company Ltd.

Library of Congress Cataloging-in-Publication Data
Bruel, Nick.
Poor Puppy / by Nick Bruel. — 1st ed.   p. cm.
"A Neal Porter book."

Summary: When Bad Kitty won't play with him, Poor Puppy has to amuse himself with an alphabetical list of toys and dreams of playing in an alphabetical list of countries.

ISBN: 978-1-59643-270-3
[1. Alphabet — Fiction.
2. Dogs — Fiction.
3. Cats — Fiction.]
I. Title.

PZ7.B82832Poo 2007
[E] — dc22
2006032191

www.roaringbrook press.com

GROCERY LIST --
MILK
EGGS
CAT FOOD!

FOR JOHN, JOHANNA + MIKAELA

Roaring Brook Press books are available for special promotions and premiums. For details contact: Director of Special Markets, Holtzbrinck Publishers

First edition September 2007
Printed in November 2010 in China by South China Printing Co. Ltd., Dongguan City, Guangdong Province
10 9 8 7 6 5 4 3

Puppy's
best
friend
is
Kitty.

But Puppy
is sad.

Kitty doesn't want to play with him today.

Poor Puppy.

Poor, poor Puppy.

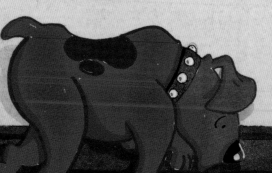

Poor, poor, poor, poor,

POOR

Puppy!

Instead of Kitty,
the only things
Puppy has to play
with are . . .

4 Dolls

5 Electric Trains

6 Finger Puppets

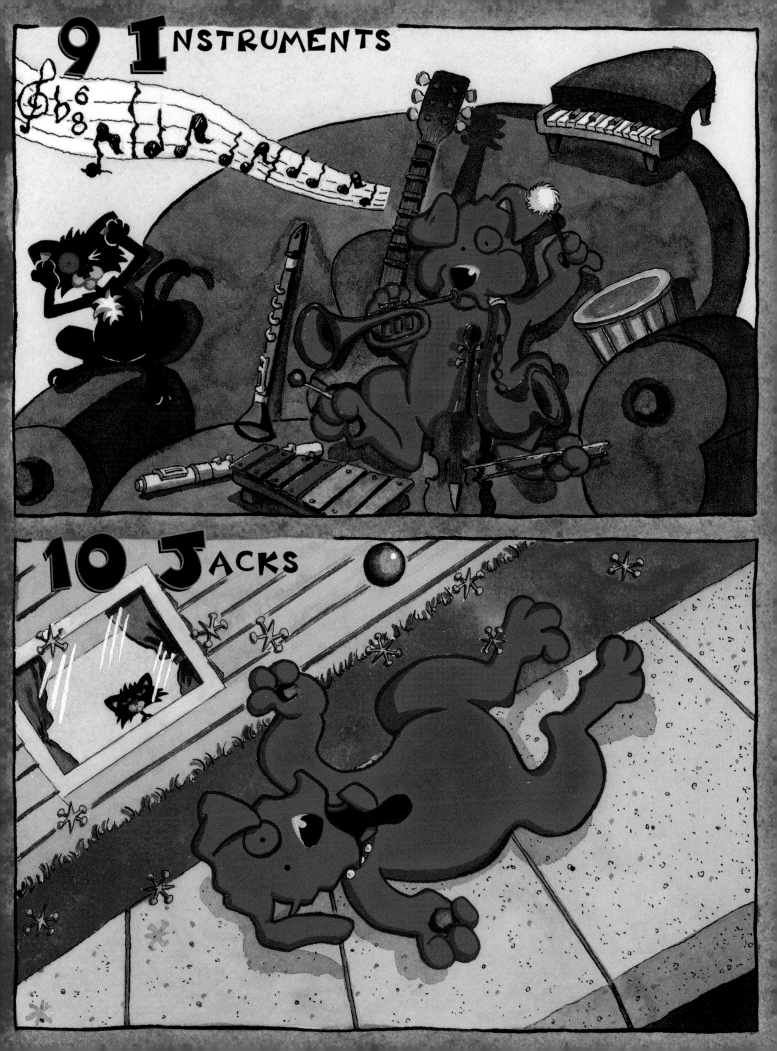

11 Kites

12 Liters of Fingerpaints

13 Marbles

14 Nutcrackers

15 Old cat toys he found under the sofa

16 Pinwheels

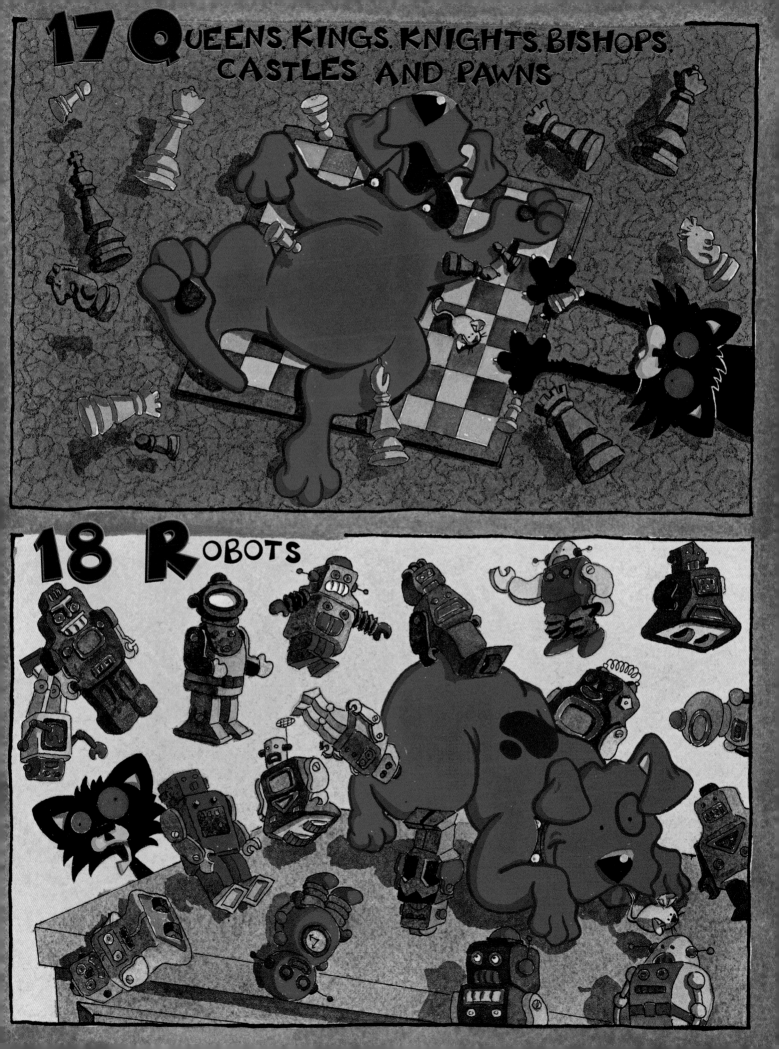

19 SOCCER BALLS

20 TEDDY BEARS

That was FUN!
But Puppy really wanted to
play with Kitty.

Poor Puppy.

Now he's so tired,
he has to take a nap.

Poor Puppy.

When Puppy naps, he dreams.

What do you think he dreams about?

He dreams about playing with Kitty, of course!

They play . . .

OLD MAID IN OMAN

PATTY-CAKE IN PERU

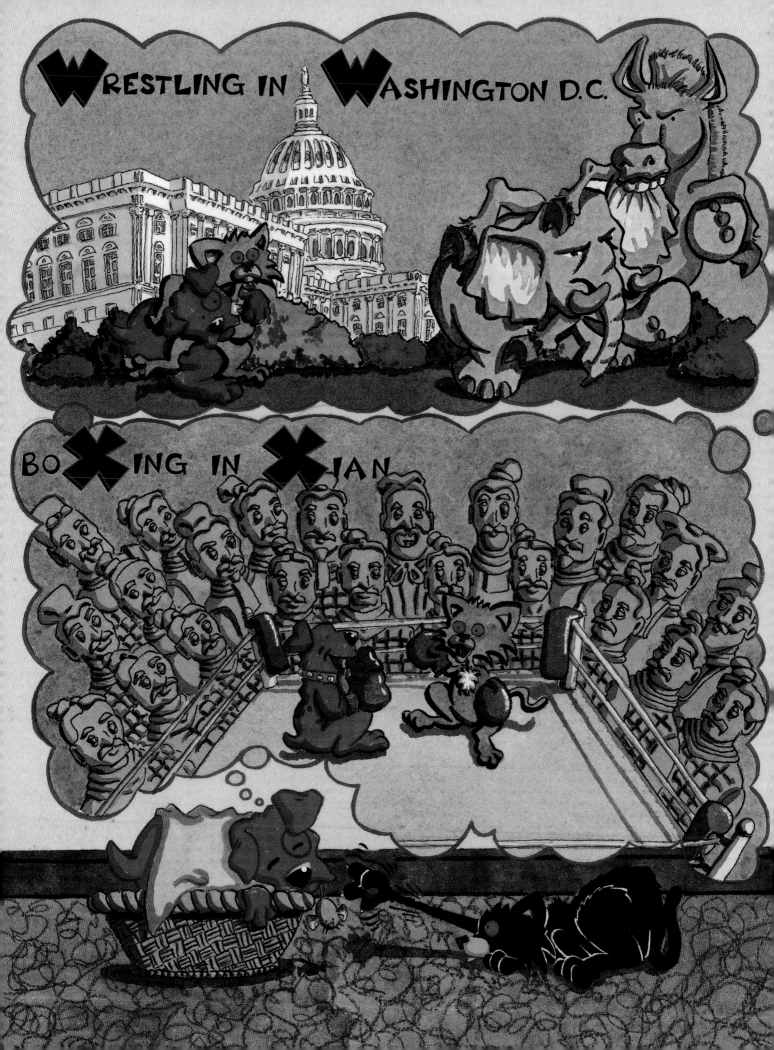

. . . Puppy wakes up.

What a great dream!
Now Puppy is so happy,
he wants to play!

And so does Kitty!

HOORAY!